FINE, FINE, FINE, FINE, FINE

FINE, FINE, FINE, FINE, FINE

STORIES

DIANE WILLIAMS

McSWEENEY'S
SAN FRANCISCO

McSWEENEY'S

This book is made possible by generous support from Xandra Coe.

Cover design by Dan McKinley.

The art on this book's cover is unsigned and was created for a romance novella published in Mexico City in the 1960s that appeared in serial form. This piece was produced using collage and gouache overpainting on illustration board, and the back reads "El Angel No. 64." The printer of these covers held on to the originals for decades, and the entire collection was recently purchased from his warehouse. Works are available from the Pardee Collection Gallery of Iowa City, and "El Angel" is provided courtesy of Diane Williams and Wolfgang Neumann.

McSweeney's and colophon are registered trademarks of McSweeney's, an independent publisher with wildly fluctuating resources.

ISBN 978-1-940450-84-1
Printed in the United States

2   4   6   8   10   9   7   5   3   1

www.mcsweeneys.net

ALSO BY DIANE WILLIAMS

*This Is About the Body, the Mind, the Soul,
the World, Time, and Fate*

*Some Sexual Success Stories Plus Other Stories
in Which God Might Choose to Appear*

The Stupefaction

Excitability: Selected Stories 1986–1996

Romancer Erector

It Was Like My Trying to Have a Tender-Hearted Nature

Vicky Swanky Is a Beauty

CONTENTS

How long will Harry Doe live?... Who will win the war?...
Will Mary Jane Brown ultimately find a husband...?

—LEO MARKUN

BEAUTY, LOVE, AND VANITY ITSELF

As usual I'd hung myself with snappy necklaces, but otherwise had given my appearance no further thought, even though I anticipated the love of a dark person who will be my source of prosperity and emotional pleasure.

Mr. Morton arrived about 7 p.m. and I said, "I owe you an explanation."

"Excellent," he replied. But when my little explanation was completed, he refused the meal I offered, saying, "You probably don't like the way I drink my soda or how I eat my olives with my fingers."

He exited at a good clip and nothing further developed from that affiliation.

The real thing did come along. Bob—Tom spent several days in June with me and I keep up with books and magazines and go forward on the funny path pursuing my vocation.

I also went outside to enjoy the fragrant odor in an Illinois town and kept to the thoroughfare that swerved near the fence where yellow roses on a tawny background are always faded out at the end of the season.

I never thought a big cloud hanging in the air would be crooked, but it was up there—gray and deranged.

Happily, in the near distance, the fence was making the most of its colonial post caps.

And isn't looking into the near distance sometimes so quaint?— as if I am re-embarking on a large number of relations or recurrent jealousies.

Poolside at the Marriott Courtyard, I was wearing what others may laugh at—the knee-length black swimsuit and the black canvas shoes—but I don't have actual belly fat, that's just my stomach muscles gone slack.

I saw three women go into the pool and when they got to the rope, they kept on walking. One woman disappeared. The other two flapped their hands.

"They don't know what the rope is," the lifeguard said. "I mean everybody knows what a rope means."

I said, "Why didn't you tell them?" and he said, "I don't speak Chinese."

I said, "They are drowning" and the lifeguard said, "You know, I think you're right."

Our eyes were on the surface of the water—the wobbling patterns of diagonals. It was a hash—nothing to look at—much like my situation—if you're not going to do anything about it.

A GRAY POTTERY HEAD

How tenderly she had arranged the gray pottery head of a woman on her mantel—the subtly revealed head of an archaic woman. It exhibits some bumps and some splits. This was a gift from the Danish gentleman who had also given her a Georg Jensen necklace in the original box.

She had been lucky in love as she understood it.

And that night—some progress to report. Something exciting afoot. She has a quarter hour more to live.

Even if she only gets to the lower roadway, she'll have to manage somehow.

Her boiled woolen cloak was wrapped around her tilting body and she was driving her car as if it were being blown away by the wind.

She had gone down this particular road to go home for years. This time she also arrived close by the familiar place, dying.

A tulip tree, tucked into a right angle formed by two planes, was brought into her view.

The police officer who inspected her dead body saw one area of damage and the pretty mother-of-pearl, gold and enamel Jensen ornament that was around her neck.

She has been associated with sex and with childbirth. No less interesting, she was a traveler on this unsophisticated country road.

Her facial features are remarkably symmetrical, expressing vigor and vulnerability.

CINCH

My back started killing me and Tamara asked what else did I want and why? Oddly, she was suddenly unenthusiastic about me and she revealed resentment, of all things, and possibilities for her revenge.

But how busy I was!—building the twelve-by-sixteen rec room at the rear of the house.

I made bedplates and cut boards. And this was the day that Tamara baked her standard sponge cake.

When I reached for a taste of the cake, she took the plate away.

So I slapped her and drilled holes for anchor bolts, used a shim to level bedplates and my half-inch nuts to secure the bedplates.

"Have I seen that before?" I asked her, for by then Tamara smoked a cigarette near the site and she was waving an arm on which slid—up and down—a bracelet of lumpy blue glass.

A beautiful beam of light—perhaps it was aqua—was produced by the sun poking through the dangles at her wrist.

And then again that woman behaved unfavorably toward me, for I had laid my hands on her small-sized, stooped back, or I had prodded her.

By the next May, Tamara had departed and Hesper, her replacement, carried a tray of old-time spring tonic for the two of us. Yet Hesper is so perfectly content to pursue me, seeing as how I expected she'd soon lose interest in the project or not have any real knack for it.

At this point we marched around the yard attentively, and I could tell from her remarks, and from how she laughed seriously, that I would not need to worry too much about her—as if I'd considered all of the pitfalls and avoided them.

There was a green glow from the thin, scratched surface of the lawn.

And there was that underlying melody when Hesper groaned because she saw the gopher hole—rather, we saw that typical mound of soil.

We had to set a cinch trap.

After you catch a gopher, you tap it headfirst, dead, right back into the hole! That's good fertilizer.

This isn't just a big joke. Pests move in from other areas and damage can occur in a short time from new ones who reinvade the world of nature.

But after I put to death a friendship, a marriage?

There are people to take their places, who move in from other areas, of course. There are people who are dedicated to the true good, who work toward this goal. There are animals that may not.

GULLS

The gulls in the wind looked to her like fruit flies or gnats. Two gulls flying suffered an in-air collision. One fell. The other briefly stood there—appearing to do next to nothing. The woman didn't think she was supposed to see that.

So how far did the injured gull fall?—for it did not show itself again.

From the ninth floor, the adults in the street looked to her like children. But who were the children that she saw meant to be?

"We'll have to knock ourselves into shape, won't we?" the

woman told her husband. She had once intended to evaluate their options for the improvement of their understanding.

She was fingering her glass that held water—the water that, of course, slides downhill when she drinks it—the water that one could say stumbles.

Now, in the back of their building beyond the river, there is a hollow—the unfilled cavity—although nobody can escape that way.

The woman went to bed that night with nothing much accomplished vis-à-vis the mysteries of daily life.

Her husband, next to her, squats carefully. Then he is on his knees above her.

He keeps his chin down, giving proper shape to what he is trying to express—his romantic attitude toward life.

TO REVIVE A PERSON IS
NO SLIGHT THING

People often wait a long time and then, like me, suddenly, they're back in the news with a changed appearance. Now I have fuzzy gray hair. I am pointing at it. It's like baby hair I am told.

Two people once said I had pretty feet.

I ripped off some leaves and clipped stem ends, with my new spouse, from a spray of fluorescent daisies he'd bought for me, and I asserted something unpleasant just then.

Yes, the flowers were cheerful with aggressive petals, but in a few days I'd hate them when they were spent.

The wrapping paper and a weedy mess had to be discarded, but first off thrust together. My job.

Who knows why the dog thought to follow me up the stairs. Tufts of the dog's fur, all around his head, serve to distinguish him. It's as if he wears a military cap. He is dour sometimes and I have been deeply moved by what I take to be the dog's deep concerns.

Often I pick him up—stop him mid-swagger. He didn't like it today and he pitched himself out of my arms.

Drawers were open in the bedroom.

Many times I feel the prickle of a nearby, unseen force I ought to pay attention to.

I turned and saw my husband standing naked, with his clothes folded in his hands.

Unbudgeable—but finally springing into massive brightness—is how I prefer to think of him.

Actually, he said in these exact words: "I don't like you very much and I don't think you're fascinating." He put his clothes on, stepped out of the room.

I walked out, too, out onto the rim of our neighborhood—into the park where I saw a lifeless rabbit—ears askew. As if prompted, it became a small waste bag with its tied-up loose ends in the air.

A girl made a spectacle of herself, also, by stabbing at her front teeth with the tines of a plastic fork. Perhaps she was prodding dental wires and brackets, while an emaciated man at her side fed rice into his mouth from a white-foam square container, at top speed, crouched—swallowing at infrequent intervals.

In came my husband to say, "Diane?" when I went home. "I am trying," I said, "to think of you in a new way. I'm not sure what—how that is."

A fire had been lighted, drinks had been set out. Raw fish had been dipped into egg and bread crumbs and then sautéed. A small can of shoe polish was still out on the kitchen counter. We both like to keep our shoes shiny.

How unlikely it was that our home was alight and that the dinner meal was served. I served it—our desideratum. The bread was dehydrated.

I planned my future—that is, what to eat first—but not yet next and last—tap, tapping.

My fork struck again lightly at several mounds of yellow vegetables.

The dog was upright, slowly turning in place, and then he settled down into the shape of a wreath—something, of course, he'd thought of himself, but the decision was never extraordinary.

And there is never any telling how long it will take my husband, if he will not hurry, to complete his dinner fare or to smooth out left-behind layers of it on the plate.

"Are you all right?" he asked me—"Finished?"

He loves spicy food, not this. My legs were stiff and my knees ached.

I gave him a nod, made no apologies. Where were his?
I didn't cry some.

I must say that our behavior is continually under review and any one error alters our prestige, but there'll be none of that *lifting up mine eyes unto the hills.*

HEAD OF A NAKED GIRL

One got an erection while driving in his car to get to her. Another got his while buying his snowblower, with her along. He's the one who taught her how to blow him and that's the one she had reassured, "You're the last person I want to antagonize!"

The men suspect her of no ill will and they've stuck by her. She's enjoyed their examinations of her backside in her bed.

And although there's no danger, one of the men had a somewhat bluff interest in her. He was handsome with dim-lit eyes. She liked to joke with him.

While she bent forward to her comfort level, at her sink, without holding her breath, she kept her mouth open. He applied himself against her and she allowed his solution to gently drain from her.

The paper she'd gathered together, and added to several times—to dry herself—was unfairly harsh—so often, such a number of times, regularly, usually.

But something more. Another man, when he stopped by, noted that things had become almost too satisfactory. He saw copies of old masters on the wall, not obvious to him on his previous visits.

"Is something wrong?" the girl asked.

As a rule, she blamed herself—for yet another perfect day.

RHAPSODY BREEZE

Her salesman had hair like a fountain on top of his head, and then it came down around at the sides of his head to just above his shoulders. He had a boy's physicalness, yet his mustache was gray and he never thanked her for the big sale.

No one would ever say of him—He has such a nice face or that he looks like such a nice man, but he had not intended to misuse her.

After all, hadn't he tried to stop her from buying one of the heaviest mattresses that she surely will regret purchasing.

That poor decision of hers is well past her now as she presses her paint roller from here to there and back while she is utter-ing little grunts that sound reasonable as she shifts her ladder.

The ceiling turns terra-cotta—the walls will be red, the door cerulean blue, the sills and window sashes kelly green. There'll be a turquoise mantel—and, for her dinner—more pleasure and change. She'll cook a strong-juiced vegetable, prepare a medley salad with many previously protected and selected things in it.

The salesman, at his home, empties a pitcher of water into a pot-ted plant that has produced several furred buds that he's been studying and waiting on—courting, really—but it's as if these future flowers intentionally thwart him. He assumes responsi-bility for their behavior.

Also, he thinks he doesn't know how to get people to do things.

He takes a cloth and wipes the greasy face of his computer. He checks his mustache in the mirror to see if it is trimmed properly.

He asks himself, What do you want to ask me? Will you look at that?

To begin with he thinks he's had enough of chewing on his mustache. The next thought after that is—What a lot of wild sprouts there are above his mouth—and he assumes responsibil-ity for their behavior. The step after that is to get his hairbrush and the scissors and to approach the real challenge, which is to steady his oscillating hand so he can aim it at the appropriate sec-tion of his face where the offensive hairs are. Then he brushes the mustache to see how unevenly he's cut it, and then it depends on how much time he has, not enough. Should he adjust the one side to match the other side?—because there is a limit. He may end up cutting off his entire mustache.

He presses his face closer to the mirror. He could not make it out, could not recognize the opportunity for bewitching himself.

LAVATORY

There had been the guest's lavatory visit—to summarize. She did so want to be comfortable then and for the rest of her life. She had been hiking her skirt and pulling down her undergarment, just trying not to fall apart.

Once back in the foyer, she brought out a gift for her host. "I tried to find something old for you to put on your mantel, but I just couldn't. I tried to find something similar to what you already have, to be on the safe side, but I couldn't."

It was difficult for the guest to comprehend easily what the other invitees were saying, because she wasn't listening carefully.

One man happened to have a son who knew her son. He had learned something of importance about her son—about his prospects. Something.

But the guest interrupted him, "I don't agree that there is a comfortable space for each of us out there and we have to find it. I think this is so wrong. It assumes there is a little environment that you can slip into and be perfectly happy. My notion is you try to do all the things you're comfortable with and eventually you will find your comfortable environment."

A man they called Mike smoked a maduro and he had a urine stain on his trouser fly. He was very attentive to the host and to his wife Melissa.

"Stop!" his wife cried, but he'd done it already—tipped the ashtray he'd used—the dimpled copper bowl—into the grate behind the fire screen. The ashes fell down nicely, sparsely. There was still some dark, sticky stuff leftover in the bowl.

The host called, "Kids! Mike! Dad and Mom!" He called these copulators to come in to dinner. In fact, this group represented a predictable array of vocations—including hard workers, worriers, travelers, and liars—defecators, of course, urinators and music makers.

PEOPLE OF THE WEEK

"She just can't hop over the ocean. She has small children," Petra said.

"I didn't think you even knew what Ethelind looked like."

"I saw her up front. I thought you saw her. Let's go see Tim."

"I don't want to see Tim. Why would I want to see Tim? Who is Anita? I want to thank Anita."

"Dale, is that you?" a woman called. It was Tim who turned, thinking that someone had mistaken him for Dale.

The damage from that misunderstanding was irremeable and Tim felt that he was standing up only on his hind legs, shaking hands with a forepaw. It was kind of rough for Tim while wearing the pair of trousers, his belt, and the shirt with the collar.

Anita took hold of Tim's necktie. "Come on, tell me that bug story again," she said. She was satisfied that nothing of much depth or subtlety would ever occur to her again.

Tim pushed her hand off of his necktie. "Where do I know you from?" he said.

Dale led the way into the dining room. He can't stand the situation—this branch of the activity.

Imogene inquired, "What was her name?"

That was Jasmine, who deals sensibly with everyone.

These are people who, owing to curious regularities, maintain high, trusted positions. They have acquired love, wealth, and fame, but they don't think they've gotten enough reward for all that.

THE ROMANTIC LIFE

"Gunther should show up and act as if he's learned something," Rohana said. "But he has a very good situation where he is—I am sure. I don't know why he'd want to come back here."

Gunther had died young and she thought he visited the house whenever she traveled. This was her explanation for why a five-hundred-pound mirror had fallen off of the wall when she was in Cannes. Gunther was to blame. And his pet dog Spark—long dead too—had trotted out of the boxwood to greet her upon her return. However, unlike Gunther, the ancient Airedale had chosen to stay on.

Aunt Rohana offered me my favorite—her red porridge specialty—a compote made from berries and served with heavy cream. "You can always cheer me up!" she said.

And, really—wasn't this a lavish new world with new and possibly better rules?—so that I would no longer be sitting along the curbing. And, I thought Rohana loved me, whereas my own mother, her sister, did not.

I tried not to pry my thoughts away from my new surroundings, because I had been left alone for a few hours—and I was almost successful.

As I was a young woman without a sexual partner—awareness of the deprivation was not half the battle—I was thinking about sex and at the same time I was moving my attention to the furniture, the fireplace—the walls and all of the doors that bore oak carvings in art nouveau.

Then I saw Gunther!—or he could have been a replica of the lost original. A small bent male figure was on the threshold of my room, close by a tripod table.

He slouched toward me and there was something that was not eager in his eyes. But nevertheless, he looked determined.

"Why don't you speak?" he said.

He was zipped into a fur-trimmed anorak—and not at all dressed properly for the hot summer season.

He kicked the table.

"Where have you been?" I asked.

"Dead," he said. He made his way into the kitchen and the dog Spark and I followed him.

He put two hands on the sink rim to begin the maneuver and next he pivoted on his heels. He pushed in the upper dishwasher tray that had been left out and was overhanging.

The dog gasped behind me. I turned—and when I turned back around Gunther was gone.

My memory is that Rohana had run an errand that day to get a chicken to roast, a box of soap, and a ball of twine.

"Oh, God! What do you want me to say?" she said, when I told her.

I stayed at Rohana's another day or two before I went home with a new backbone for my plodding along.

Sudden sounds didn't frighten me and I didn't mind the sense of being stared at when I was alone.

Rohana has a nerve condition now, such that if she sits still and doesn't move her left foot, she is fine. Otherwise she needs to take a lot of pain medication.

And as Gunther has done—I have shown up in certain places with a bang. And when I come into rooms, it's surely a relief to one and all that I am helpful.

I feel there is so much yet to explore about how people experience a "pull" toward anyone.

THE GREAT PASSION
AND ITS CONTEXT

She bears the problems inherent in her circumstance that are not suddenly in short supply and she sways while guessing who really looks at her impatiently while she faces all of the faces—the multiple rows of the pairs of persons—the prime examples in the train aisle.

She has her shoes back on, because she had to get up to dispose of her lunchtime detritus. But fortunately she did not fall onto the passenger next to her, that man, when she returned.

They are passing through a city center with turn-of-thecentury-style lanterns and ice skaters who put their feet down, somewhat decisively, all over a rink!

Some of their legs are bowed and there are the curvilinear, stylized profiles of their legs exemplifying natural organic forms, but they're none of them hobbling.

This woman's foot was recently injured and many weeks' rest were required before she had the rapture of standing on it—in strict accordance with the doctor's instructions.

Oh, cover my mouth!—she thinks, as her wet nose, while she coughs, finds her forearm. And although she is usually an irate parent, she has her share of lovesick feelings, especially during intervals of freedom from her toddlers, such as this one.

She feels the onset of arousal, of genital swelling that is triggered by no one in particular and she has the inability to think normally.

What's still to come?—a warm flat landscape?—a shallow swimming pool?—the complete ruin of her health?—her absolute devotion to anyone?

The top of the woman's foot is still puffy and she has had quarrels at home every day this week and she goes to sleep distraught.

With dexterity, she had managed the bundling of her lunchtime cardboard tray, some cellophane and the napkin and a waxy cup.

Children, who belong to another woman three rows up ahead, are singing a duet—two boys—in unison, and then in contrary motion. They offer their share of resistance to you name it!—in a remote and difficult key, and in poor taste artistically.

SPECIALIST

"For a blue sky, that blue's a bit dark, don't you think? And the sea's a bit too choppy," I said, "for that dog to be dashing into it."

"You mean the man threw something into the water?" my son said. "That's why the dog jumped in?"

An hour passed. Why not say twenty years?

In the Green Room, I had fortunately ordered Frenched Chicken Breast—Chocolate Napoleon.

And at a great height—up on a balcony, as I readied to

depart—a pianist began his version of Cole Porter's "Katie Went to Haiti." I waved to him.

He nodded, likely pleased by the attention, but it was hard to tell—for only his radiant pate was made visible by a tiny ceiling light.

To my surprise, the air in the street was too hot to give pleasure and a cyclist was mistakenly on the sidewalk.

The cyclist hit me, and it's vile after my life ends in the afterlife. Lots of incense, resin, apes, and giraffe-tails—all acquired tastes. I don't like that kind of thing.

THE POET

She carves with a sharply scalloped steel blade, makes slices across the top of a long, broad loaf of yeasted bread for the dog who begs and there's a cat there, too.

She holds the loaf against her breast and presses it up under her chin. But this is no violin! Won't she sever her head?

AT A PERIOD OF
EXCEPTIONAL DULLNESS

The influence of the early evening's sunset was much less bloody inside of the salon, spreading itself like red smoke or like a slowly moving red fog, unbounded.

Yet, Mrs. Farquhar's hair was nearly bloodred, and it behaved like dry hair.

The hairdresser lifted a clump of it, dropped it. To soften it, she reached for her leave-in detangler.

She looked for more signs of neglect, the thread connections that could come to light. She said, "It's all broken. It's much worse."

The haircut trickled along, and it would take a long time.

But how terribly unhappy Mrs. Farquhar was. She must not have been adaptable to something else much more serious in particular.

However, the tea she had been served had the tang of the dirty lake of her childhood that she remembered swallowing large amounts of while swimming, and she wore the shop's black Betty Dain easy-to-wear client wrap robe.

The full view of Mrs. Farquhar's face and of her hair in the mirror was a trial for both of them.

Nonetheless, the hairdresser preened. She wore an elite Betty Dain gown, too.

Later she tidied up and by breakfast time, at home, the next morning—the hairdresser was alone, wedged between her chair and the table. There was a plastic plate in front of her and a ceramic mug. These both had glossy surfaces—impenetrable, opaque.

She removed her solitaire pearl finger ring, put it onto the plate.

Through the window she saw her pruned shrubbery, a narrow green lawn, no trees.

She believed it was her duty to size these things up.

What was it that she did or did not admire? It was a question of her upsetting something.

HEAD OF THE BIG MAN

The family was blessed with more self-confidence than most of us have and with a great lawn, with arbors and beds of flowers, and with a fountain in the shape of a sun at the south end. It is not our purpose to say anything imprecise about their scheme, how they had gotten on with tufted and fringed furniture, with their little tables, a parquet floor, a bean pot.

The walls inside of this country house were amber-colored where they entertained quite formally—until the old mansion was destroyed.

It was a shapely shingle-style house, with bulbous posts.

But what kind of confident people behave poorly by not being confident enough?

Let us examine the case.

Eldrida Cupit had given birth to four children. Three of these and their father drowned trying to cross the Quesnel River in a boat. She later married Mr. Cupit and had many more children. "Imp," as she was known, was famous for her fresh peach sour cream pie, her steak shortcake, and more significantly for her élan.

People often saw her husband Blade on the street and he not only was polite, but he invited many personally to his home to hear about his rough riding days and his numerous good works.

In her later years, Mrs. Cupit dressed slowly for dinner and did not intend nor want to see anyone, except for her husband at dinner.

Frequently her husband left the table before she arrived and then edged himself up the back stairs.

He began to drink and lost all of his money after his wife died.

Often, as in this tale, a downpour with thunder and lightning is sufficiently full-bodied to get somebody's whole attention. In one such storm Mr. Cupit had a vision of his wife. Her clothing was not exactly cut to fit and she showed no sign of affection. "Well, act like you're not going up a hill," his wife said, "but you're still going to go up it!"

For a while, after their deaths, their residence was open to tourists who were apt to get exhausted touring it.

The diamond-shaped hall, placed in the center—its

dimensions and spaciousness were rooted, were grounded as if the hall was growing as an ample area. It was finished in mahogany. The dominant message here being: "Looks like one of you splurged!"

None of this would have been possible without the involvement of morally strong, intelligent people who were then spent.

Young farmers and rural characters, obstetrical nurses, scholars, clergy—all the rest!—will have their great hopes realized more often than not—unless I decide to tell their stories.

LIVING DELUXE

True! Yes! Mother always gave me a tribute with a sigh. I was her favorite, and that was another reason I took money from her that rightfully belonged to my sister and my brother.

My mother knew I needed to be a person with flair and I can be. It may require a little time.

No lack of courage could have caused me to turn away from a day laborer on the foot pavement who sneezed a larger-than-life-size sneeze with an open mouth. Then he crossed himself multiple times, as I went by him.

It pained me to hold my breath while outdistancing him, and I wondered how far I'd need to go to keep free of any noxious air. I thought briefly I might count out the accurate, necessary number of cubic feet or yards.

But I was restful during a letup in the late afternoon, when my sister visited me. Her metal necklace caught at my shawl collar and it pulled loose a thread as I embraced her.

Her appearance needed some repair, too.

She is Liz Munson. She is a judge! She decides whether people live or die!

She declined a drink but ate a few of the hemp seeds I'd left out in my hors d'oeuvre dish.

"How is Maurice?" I said. "Did that one end?"

"He's with the boys," she said, and then took a pause to round out her lungs to their capacity.

Henry the cat put his paws up on me and called out a critical remark. Then he made his other noise that is tinged with bitterness. He is sand color in the style of the day with cement accents.

Liz's Henry is black chestnut.

I'll make no attempt to explain a cat's problems that are basic to all cats—schemes that are unrealistic.

I held tightly, for an instant, on to Henry's tail, when he moved to go far afield, for his suffering and his sacrifice—although the cat's tail is a branch that refuses to break.

Henry had charm once upon a time. Now he wastes it stalking. "Stay and eat with me, Liz."

"Oh, dear," she said.

What had she come for?

My sister picked up a piece of bric-a-brac that was on the console and put it into the unimpressive realm of her handbag. What I call a toy—what she took—was mine, never Mother's: a leaden mammal of some sort, with horns.

Oddly, Liz has never noticed here her ten-pounder da Vinci omnibus with its gravure illustrations, its spine sensationally exhibited on a shelf, that bears this inscription on the frontispiece: *To Liʒ and Neville, with best wishes for a happy life in a world of friendship and guʒ.* (That last was illegible.) *Signed Stephen and Lil Cole.*

Leonardo may not have founded science, but I learned from him that genius does not bog down.

I lit the stove top and put water on to boil and next poured in baby peas. I made parallel straight rules—incisions in the chunk of Gruyere. The water foamed in the pot and I filled a rare antique potato basket with New York rye.

"You are a wonder," my sister said. "I am not after your food. I want to bring you bad luck."

"No harm done!" I said.

The peas had cooked and cooled. I prepared a pea and cheese stuffed-tomato salad. Enough for two.

My visitor was nagging at me, which was hurtful to the pride I intend to take along with me into my future.

And just where am I now?

I live near a dip in the suburbs. Some would call this a ravine—which I make visible at night with floodlights.

I believe it demands cunning enterprise on my part to reveal the fancywork of bare winter poplar and oak, maple and ash. I saw a sycamore tree bent at more than fifteen degrees from vertical!

My dining table is only nominally illuminated, so that our hands and our arms and Liz's face became quickly—sickly. Unaccountably, she had sat herself right across from me.

My sister sneezed and put her hand to her mouth in time.

"God bless you," I said.

She sneezed again rather more sloppily and that reminded me of a joke. She underwent yet another sudden, spasmodic action—and this time she did not try to keep her bacteria back.

My harrier removed two handmade beeswax candles from their brass serpent candleholders on her way out.

She yelled my name—"Ola!"—and I turned away for relief—aiming to sit in my wingback rather than the lounge chair.

I saw the downed sycamore through the pane, the suggestion of a sky far away, and some of the sharply peaked trees straining to bend or to unbend, or at least to shed their shapes, or to be somewhat more neatly executed.

Very well. I took from my family one hundred thousand dollars—say fifty thousand. Say it was three million. It was thirty-five thousand!—forty. It was two hundred dollars.

There was aggravated tapping near the tall wraparound window.

By way of conclusion—I need to say I had divided a pack of gems between Liz and myself. In doing this, I'd forgotten my brother. The nonpareils, I wear in my ears.

There was that tapping again—a repeated and demonic phrase—and the repellent sight of animals through the glass.

They are my very own public property.

Such bollixed and blank expressions.

These flocks and herds and creeping things! Don't you think they all go to work so wretchedly for what then never amounts to *a feast for the soul?*

How to live: there are two factors to consider—my husband says there are five!—and one of them puts me into a rage.

My fingers are graceful when I lay the table. My voice is clear when I speak. For God's sake! For the Lord's got such style, such originality and boldness.

PERSONAL DETAILS

On the avenue, I was unavoidably stuck inside of an uproar when the wind locked itself in front of my face.

Nevertheless, I had a smeary view of a child in the whirlwind who was walking backward. He was carrying his jacket instead of wearing it. And he kicked up his feet with such aptitude.

In a luncheonette that I took cover in, I overheard, "Yes, I do mind..."—this, while I was raising and rearranging memories of many people's personal details, tryst locales, endearments— faces, genitalia, like Jimmy T's, or Lee's, which I pine for.

This is regular work with regular work hours that I do.

Through the windowpane of the coffee shop, I could see clearly into a hair salon across the street where two men—both with hairbrushes and small, handheld dryers—together—downstroked the mane of a cloaked woman.

The men were performing feats of legerdemain. Streamers sprang up around her head, as if snakes or dragons were busy eating their own tails.

And then, weighing down her shoulders, there was the golden hoard—for future use—of bullshit.

FLYING THINGS

The Bucky's waitress says she is happy to have back that amorous part of her life and that this makes her less of a Plainer Jane.

And, with an old man named Humphrey, she says she's made a pretty bargain.

Today she said, "I'll take some of this, too!" and she took a gulp of my water.

And we enjoy laughing about the poor hot beverages she serves and about our divorced husbands. Although my partner in marriage, Ray, was nobody to laugh about—Ellie always says she'll clear the decks to ignore that.

The surrogate judge I work for, Maxine Joe, was also run over and she was really flattened, but she is doing so much better. She is the kind of gold you see in a museum and she is extremely dedicated and she works hard.

Maxine took papers out of my hands and she said, "Can you postpone?" She meant my trip to Hot Springs.

It was a warmish day—mild. There were flies in the office. I got down on my knees to chase one.

Does a fly reminisce about a good time?—thinking, I'll do that again tomorrow. It had been sitting on my hand for a moment. Does it plan to go into a different room and sit on a sleeve, or a desk, or a wall? Is it thinking, I'll hook onto something and get attached there long enough to get killed?

I had noticed today a man running in the park, no shirt, no socks. He did have shorts on. Maxine had brought in hyacinths and she said she had met a new man. It strikes me how, uh, how everyone is looking for a partner, wondering, What now?

It is remarkable—every person! This woman who is married—in our office—can now approach Hugh the office manager. Even this young Australian boy is starting to have an interest in Dyana.

But life isn't quite like that.

HOW BLOWN UP

A server making noisy cascades was busy refilling their glasses with ice water from a tall pitcher.

That's what it was like in there—all peppy! Wouldn't you know it? It had not been a period of decline.

Having made up her mind, "Why—excuse me," the woman said peremptorily. She left the café and stepped out into the rain. She was not scaled down or reversed in her views.

There was a car just outside that she stepped into. No daylight any longer.

She rode in the taxicab toward a higher order on account of the movement of her thought.

Here's the spot!

We shall see!

Do you know how the animals got their tails? How the lesser gods came into the world?

The longer this goddess lives, the more she shakes her tail— or pulls on it with all her strength.

SIGH

Why would anyone be fearful that the man might become distressed or that he might lose his temper in their bedroom? He is a calm man by nature and not liable to break anything really nice by accident.

He had decided to disrobe in there—where they keep their Polish woman statuette and the fish dish they use for loose coins.

To be civilized, this man had asked to meet with his wife's new husband.

The three drank tea together, impromptu, from souvenir mugs and paid mind to one another's questions and the uninformative replies. Next, the man had stepped into their bedroom, towing his roller board, after inquiring if he could change into more comfortable clothes in preparation for his travel. He said he'd be leaving soon enough—flying into the northeast corridor that he'd heard was an absolute quagmire. Hard rain had been falling freely and for several days. In addition, now they were suffering occasional sleet. The pressure, the moisture, and the black clouds were progressing. This is a humid, continental climate in turmoil.

"You're wearing that?" the wife said, when the man reemerged in Spandex fitness apparel.

"We found it in Two Dot! You don't remember?" he said—fondly patting lightly his own chest. "It's breathable. It's stretchable."

"I thought it was in Geraldine," the wife said.

"But look here, maybe you should stay the night," the new husband said. He offered seed cake and coffee—the mild and friendly kind—this time, to drink.

"What are you doing?" said the wife—for her husband's hands were filled with the sugar bowl and the creamer and several cups were swinging from his fingers by their ears.

All so beautifully turned out, the dishes found the table's surface safely. These were specimens of the most romantic china service. The gilding was very good—the glaze finely crazed. There were hand-painted sprays on an apple-green ground.

"I hope you are a comfort to her," the man said, "and that you show good sense. Because this is what it is—doesn't everybody have to take care of Tasha?" He did not refer to her sex behavior and instead spoke generally about the dell they had once lived in and lunged silently at his disappointment that he could no longer touch his former wife. He extolled the mountain town where the wife had often reflected that looking up and out, say, over at an elevated ridge—was to her advantage.

Now she resided in this flatter state in an apartment on the third floor across from the church—from where she could see its spire.

Her glance often ran recklessly toward it, as if spurting over a rim, or through a spout.

The chancel and the sanctuary had lately been under ugly scaffolding. A few years back, one of the two aisle rose windows had been carried away for restoration and had not been returned yet.

Fortunately, the inner-draw draperies of the couple's window facing the church were made of cheerful chintz.

"It wouldn't surprise me if I stayed," the man said. "Well, sure, yes, absolutely, you bet!" he said. "I'm a little nervous."

He prepared to eat by sitting down and stressing his jaws with a big smile.

His cheeks are elongated and hollow—his brow highly peaked. His face is not difficult to explain—it's cathedral-like.

The new husband's whole head has an unfinished look that promises to work out well. Whereas the wife's furrowed face—some have said—shows heavy evidence of deception and is cause for alarm.

Right then, in front of them, the woman uncapped a tube of gel ointment and applied a dab of it under a long fingernail. Next she opened a cellophane packet from which she withdrew a cracker that produced plenty of crumbs.

The husband told the man, "Surely you'd be welcome to stay!"

As the wife mopped up her particles and the traces, she spoke somewhat rudely to the man and also to her husband.

"I went somewhere…" the man said, expanding on a point. Hadn't he been molded to better express himself?

A small object's overall smallness on a shelf caught his eye—a round-bodied jar of free-blown glass whose neck was straight, that had flat shoulders—a flask he would not get to smash! It was streaked with permanent crimson and cold black. It had about it the real suggestion of the softness of human flesh.

"Did you imagine me the way I am?" the man asked the new husband, who answered no.

"What do you mean?"

"But I am not against you," the husband said.

"Say a little more."

Sirens in the street produced a brief, headstrong fugue.

"Say a little more," said the man.

The husband got up from his chair. Why should anyone be fearful of his certain combinations of words, narrowly spaced?

The husband gave himself ample time to speak.

No gross vices were explored. His is not the voice of a man in the pulpit. No personal impulses were defined or analyzed.

He did deliver a slovenly interrogatory.

He went uphill, downhill with—"Wah-aaaaaaaat waaahz it ligh-ike, with herrrrrrrrr-rah, for you-ooooooo—?"

That's all that he was saying.

Nothing seemed to want to end it.

THERE IS ALWAYS A HESITATION BEFORE TURNING IN A FINISHED JOB

Beneath his coat, when I first met him, his shirt had seemed to have broken out into an inflammation—into a lavish plaid or a strong enough checkered pattern.

There was the stretch of time when my future materialized on account of Dan.

We fried things on the stove top and made coffee. Formerly, I had been disabled and chilled, the usual story—so then the hamburgers had become fun.

Dan was doing the job of keeping us together and he was

creating a little garden at the back of the house and the garden was extending onto the beach and the garden didn't have any grass to speak of, but we had this vision of growing things there. There was a daisy we were trying to grow. There was another flower that looked like an artichoke, but it was not only to be a garden of landscape plantings. It was supposed to be equal to our worth.

One day when we were out in the garden, a dog that had been chasing a rabbit came up to us. Dan said hello and we kept that dog. It was a tan dog and it was a mix of the best available species and the dog was trembling. He had that look in his eyes. He had the heart to do any work that was necessary, but we had nothing for him to do. And I was struck by how the dog was featuring so prominently. For instance, we might think to go someplace, but would the dog like it?

The dog had his leisure hours and Dan and I had been together longer than I expected and I was all tired out because we had indulged ourselves in every desire.

Although, occasionally, we still had a lustrous sunny day with lots of time in it, more than usual.

These days, when we tie up the dog in the yard we can barely bend to weed.

The weeds and the dead flowers—clumps—are like the stacks of our used dishes with the dribs of jelly and bite-marked bread crusts that are hardly ever put away.

So how much more describing is necessary to assess if we're done expecting something even more fortunate to turn up?

I was stepping into a corridor. It was empty except for Dan. He moved backward awkwardly, but then his face rose toward me like a steel magnet and it landed on my face with a bump. He has an enormous head and pale-pigmented skin.

I ran into him again later.

And then there was a long, long time without my seeing another human being.

And after the last years were over, we were dead.

THE MERMAID POSE

The mother had fought a small cause to prevent the little girl from sticking her hand into the pond to try to catch a fish, but the child fell in and went under. Which of them did the wrong thing?

The father wrapped his hands around the crying child's neck as he lifted her up and out and the mother shook droplets from the wetted front of her own skirt.

A rose of Sharon—like an old Chinese, hand-painted lacquer screen—obscured the sight of anything more of them, as the group left. But the mother, I could hear her saying—"The what? I will not!"

But to get back to the pond!—we were at the Burnett Fountain in the Conservatory Garden where a bronze boy toots on a flute at the feet of a bronze girl who holds her overflowing bowl high.

Legs together—the boy reclines in a mermaid pose—and people in other mermaid poses had been taking turns being photographed on the stone pavers at the edge of the reflecting pool that was filled with the blue lilies and the fish.

I also lowered myself so that I was elongated and bent at the waist.

I watched a creamy madcap one ploughing among the others that were, most of them, too good to be true.

I felt an unimaginable touch. Oh, to be sweetly signaled.

A hand pressed against my back. "Come along, Kitty. We're late. You wanted a bath."

He kissed his fingers in tribute to me as I turned. And I got up with slow progress, trying for a look of extreme gladness, brushing off the back of my clothing.

A dead or disabled raccoon on the sidewalk, near the hospital, en route home, was attracting several lookers-on—partially on its side—with its legs opened up like scissor blades.

We've heard these animals in the trees and guessed what they were doing up there that always sounds so beyond the pale.

This was just going to be a sponge bath, God willing.

"You're clean enough already," my husband said.

So that was dear of him and the lineaments of his face are

stamped with his best intentions whether he has any of those or not.

I am teal and gray and added colors. I've done nothing to hide the ugliness of my elderly body. And let others regret that my character has no allure, because I am worn-out with that also.

We have a roll-top bathtub I had stepped into. I tried to sit. I was angled painfully and wedged on top of one foot—as if I am intent to prove the impossible—that I don't fit in.

GREED

Each child had a claim to a pile of jewelry when my paternal grandmother died—and how did they determine who was to have which pile?

The heirs were sent into an adjacent room and a trustee called out loudly enough to be heard by all of them—"Who will have this pile?"

My father said he shouted—"August Wilhelm will have this pile!"

Thus, my mother eventually received two gem-set rings that she wore as a pair until she achieved an advanced age and then she amalgamated the two of them into one—so that the diamonds and the sapphires were impressively bulked together.

I had to have it. It was a phantasmagoria. I selected it after my mother's death, not because I liked it, but because it offers the memory of my mother and of the awkward, temporarily placed cold comfort that she gave me.

It's hard to believe that our affair was so long ago.

CLARINDA

This seemed to be my chance. He was obviously—I have tried not to focus on that quality. Although this was not Providence protruding into my life and sticking its big hand out in a hello.

He said, "This happens to me all of the time! Can you help me? You look just like the woman on the bus who was sitting across from me, except for the hair. I have to get something for my daughter. Should I buy TRESemmé?"

"Buy this one," I said. "I am sure your daughter would like something fancy."

Then the man said, "I smell a bakery."

"You said, 'I smell a bakery'?"

"Yes."

"I smell it, too."

"I hate it!" the man said.

"You said you hate it?"

We must have talked for many minutes more about his daughter, and after that I bought plain bond paper and a packet of rubber bands.

I wish he had seemed genuinely impressed by me.

As to the life he was leading, he said there was no wife.

I have always thought I was a careful person, but apparently I can surprise myself.

One aspect of the whole situation is that it would soon seem to be normal.

We now sleep in the same bed, drink one or two glasses of neat whiskey before dinner.

He's remained with me in my house and so has Clarinda.

Clarinda's a flower that's growing that we cannot gather.

She's not a child and she holds an important position here.

I have forgotten that the man is her father. That is sad to say and sad to hear. I consider her to be my husband's much younger and his better partner—for the pair of them scorn very similar things.

Often when I make the beds before I start supper, I can forget my family troubles that are unfunny or enigmatic. But soon they come back to me, as if in secret I'd had a coughing fit.

Such misfortunes are like the common corn cockle flowers on the fabric of my wing chairs. Never delicate—the way they've lasted—and isn't it my task to admire them? Didn't I select it?— that chintz—with slight reluctance, but unguardedly.

THE SKOL

In the ocean, Mrs. Clavey decided to advance on foot at shoulder-high depth. A tiny swallow of the water coincided with her deliberation. It tasted like a cold, salted variety of her favorite payang congou tea. She didn't intend to drink more, but she did drink—more.

THE THICKENING WISH

Typically, he walks far enough north so that he sees the bridge and he appears to be so casual as he passes objects, the people, rusticated arcades, and heavy keystones.

Here's how it is—he had just gotten as far as Childs & Son Excavation Company, which has a colonnaded façade.

His wife, back at home, sat in front of their hole-in-the-wall fireplace.

If her husband is delayed, she'll prepare for herself a nice shirred egg.

Has he anything in mind when he nears Mitchell's Sheet Metal and the Nelson Fuel Company?

You have got a lot of nerve! comes to mind. Somebody in his childhood said that frequently, but who was it who said it?

His wife is thinking, *I am usually in a rush, but I am not in a rush today.*

She stows a spool of thread and a needle threaded with the thread. And didn't she put away her ring? It had been prized and placid on the bureau top, with its many little rough points—the prongs—that in the course of time had never gone and worn themselves down smoothly.

This is how her husband's feet move his body—it's a spring-like action.

His wife hunts for more objects to put away. Many are made of cheap metal—boat-shaped or cube-shaped.

She enjoys their real fireplace, sitting by it, studying the in-and-out curve of it and the projecting stub of its mantel.

She tells herself, "Take all the time to clean up that you need."

By chance, her husband has not yet come up against the bridge he seeks—but he has seen many towers and domes, porches and arches and doors, and he always enjoys the step-gabled buildings in the old town.

Then at last, he sees the bridge that seems to him to be sinking. The bridge has become a boob, or a drunk, or a bum.

His wife puts an egg into a greased custard cup, dots it with butter, salt and pepper, and a drop of milk. She slides the egg—which had spent nearly the entirety of its life stone-cold and refrigerated—into the hot oven.

Her husband is now uncomprehending. The road he'd been on was pointing toward the bridge, so now how did the road suddenly take a sharp turn away from the bridge and head over toward this warehouse?

His wife begins to eat, but she cannot swallow.

You blockhead, you ass!

And her husband is back at the business of piling up the sights that have been left lying around.

Typically, her husband has had an air of daring while he attempts—at each important stage of the trek—to take everything in.

LAMB CHOPS, COD

She had stopped insisting that they have heart-to-heart conversations, but for stranded people, they had these nice moments together, and he had his professional enjoyment at the newspaper. He approved the issues there with a scientific mind and he made quite a contribution. He was a consultant in the field of efficiency.

She should have appreciated that, I guess. I don't know—she felt lonely.

After dinner, he would go into his room and sometimes read or do his engraving or follow up on his stamp collection or solve math problems from that year's baccalaureate examination. Once he told me that once a year he reread *Our Man in Havana*. It had something to do with Havana. You know—petty things—I guess my mother wanted full attention, not for him to have private time by himself. I don't know what my mother did when she was in her room. She was working. She was working a lot. She devoted herself to family matters, making trouble. But I am convinced that she did love him extremely and after he died she said that that was the fact.

Then they had golf together and they did trips. There was a French newspaper that would invite him to solve a technical problem. He was amazing that way.

They would playact around the occasion of having dinner. I'm not sure, but I'm afraid that they did it for every dinner. She would put on her best gown and wear the diamond ornament, which she felt free to pin anywhere on her garment if it was necessary for the brooch to cover up a soiled spot.

He wore black lacquer pumps, silk stockings that went up under the knees. His breeches were tied under the knees and he would have tails and white tie on. My mother would provide the basic meal—cod or lamb chops. He would provide—he loved to go to the store that was similar to Fortnum and Mason and buy smoked salmon, cheese, fruit in season, asparagus. They had cocktails at five o'clock. They would listen to the news and then they'd sit down to the table, light the candles. They would have their little feast together. Then after the meal, he'd sit down and do work in his room. His French was very good, so sometimes he translated manuals from French or the other way around. And before bedtime, they'd have a cup of tea together with a cookie. He loved an existence of this kind and to eat food.

He died while he was still glossy and smooth at the dinner table between the fish with dill—a great favorite—outstanding with butter—and the boiled blue plum dumplings.

OF THE TRUE AND FINAL GOOD

The gimcracks were set out on a jutting surface and the woman listened to the indoor crowd that made the sound of a storm in a dry forest.

Upon entering the mansion—referred to as "the castle" by the locals at that time—she saw the carvings in wood and in stone—and among them a white wolf with an open mouth, made from white limestone.

There was a broad blown cry from the woman that expressed her satisfaction.

By contrast, a man and a boy found the air inside difficult

to breathe and they did not view the staircase or the urns in the niches as among the finest in the world. Nor had they walked in there with the notion that *this will do*.

But other people arrived who could be benefited by observing the luxury—so that the big place didn't rub them the wrong way.

The woman eyed swords and sabers hung on the wall, all exceptional. Next to these was an oil painting in a bulky frame featuring a copper pot and eucalyptus leaves.

The woman stayed briefly in a location close by it.

The true state of things inside of the painting was unclear. The painting needed cleaning. The woman could not sufficiently experience either the fragrance of the leaves or the copper pot's heavenly glow.

"Oh, sorry!" the man with his boy said to the woman.

Something had startled him also. He was a thin little man who held his face in his hands. "I don't like this place do you?" he said.

He didn't approach too closely. But the woman reached out and laid a hand on his arm and she gripped it.

Then both of her hands were pulling at his sleeve.

People who saw her putting a lot of effort into it wondered why.

She was carefully fashioned, vivid and polished, but should her desired result fail to be obtained—she'll fade.

GLIMPSES OF MRS. WILLIAMS

I admired her that she withdrew herself before her presence became annoying, but she was definitely putting herself forward to be available and friendly.

She remembered our names and our aggravations and she gently rapped on my husband's shoulder to inquire if his rotator cuff problem had been remedied.

Well, I was impressed by that. This is my mother we are talking about!

But on a personal note, how shall I say?—she carried herself with grace.

She liked to wear this loosely knotted scarf, with a loop forward and with a knot, and with the ends of it drooping down her back.

I especially admired her odd selection of teacups and coffee cups and, I think, only once did I have a repeat presentation of a certain Denby Monsoon Veronica.

They were all very attractive—the cups—very flowerful, and the best of them had rims that would turn outward slightly in order to appear more than willing to release the tea.

There were plenty of pitchers and bowls and artwork, but their abundance never reached the level of hemming us in.

And oh, yes, there was one especially unusual amenity in the bedroom that we used—the tiny background noisemaker—that amongst its many other promises pledged it could sedate babies.

So you can understand, then, what we were doing—we were expecting benefits while visiting Mrs. Williams—my mother—for a few weeks.

She said, "Now we can walk and hold our coffee—" as she guided us to our room one Sunday, where there was the cross-eyed Sphinx that I love to get to see, with a ground-down nose, framed in gold.

Only she did keep saying, "I am so happy about that!"

Because I couldn't be happy about any of the things she said she was so happy about and now I don't remember what those things were.

But the fact that her citrus plant, when I watered it for her, had seemed to pull up its skirt to expose its private parts—does seem worth the mention.

We heard her go into her own room. Then she opened and came through our bedroom's louvered door with her complaint and where he could, my husband sat my mother down.

"What can we do?" we said.

"Call Jim! Hope for the best!" she said. "Do you have Jim's number?"

We summoned Jim who wore a long black coat when he arrived, and Mother went crazy, but just as soon as Jim took the coat off, she was fine.

"Oh, she's so worried!" Jim said. But Jim had had to plead with her, "What kind of calculation is this?"

"Now, you're going?" Mother said. "Write it down!"

In large, over-styled lettering, Jim offered his instructions that were sound.

There were other local personalities who, however, never showed up—Janis Schlitz, Marilyn Issidorides, and the Dufferins—Mother's neighbors.

I find I have an all-around vigilance. All of the time, I expect to be reached out to, by a particular person, at a particular time.

Today, a small woman—built like a small, strong man with pitted skin—said, "Gimme a cigarette. I doan like to ask."

I was on foot on my way to the food mart. The woman was folding her hands over her belly, not just clasping her hands— she was braiding her arms, terminating them in the hand clasp with some energy and leaning over to accommodate the weight of her arms and of her hands, and at the same time attempting a dainty pose by placing her legs in a dancer's position—in which the two legs were close to one another.

I was impressed by that. And when she came over to me I hoped that she would withdraw her presence before it became annoying, but she was definitely putting herself forward to be friendly and she was definitely in full progress. Perhaps she was having a mild attack—expecting me to be genial and gentle—well—at least well behaved.

It seemed to me as if there was an excellent impression I had made here in my favor.

GIRL WITH A PENCIL

The girl's predilection is to trace her hand with a pencil on a piece of paper.

The mother made a rule that her daughter was responsible for something. And what could that be?—to be sulky and disappointed?—to be heavy and club-like? To be backward?

When the child finished her early education, she drew a picture of her future that consisted of a pair of legs, column-shaped, and just above them, the hem of a skirt in bright orange. The legs were decorated—as if wrapped in wallpaper—in pastel blue with red posies and their green leaves. The shoes were clumpy, earthy.

But about the child's later life, how did she fare?

The child showed her picture to her mother.

"And where is her head?" her mother said. "I see legs!" she pointed. "Shoes."

It was just a few words, but more than the child needed to consider.

The child was handed more paper.

And so was invented a kind of brute—a brunette with long-ish hair, who must love her enemies—who acts responsibly.

PERFORM SMALL TASKS

"One second!" I said—for everything can go cold in a day or hot. For a man like me, there's an on-and-off bulb that does the deciding.

I had to find a red, little glowing button—that I was able to find—that was on a timer switch, to get more light on. The furniture—like worn-out stumps sticking up—had turned into shadows.

I could then see her better—the woman I had settled upon to have intermittent leisure with—Evangeline. How clean she was and how calm. I saw clearly the receptacle for logs by the fireplace filled with firewood that I knew to be far too fine for a fire.

It takes some ability to get close to the extraordinary in life, and I was at the peak of my ability back then.

Back then, Evangeline had informed me that her eldest son, having survived into adulthood, had returned to the States.

I heard the click upon his entry and saw the jump of the flat door.

The boy's girlish mother—who could look secretive with plans wherever you put her—withdrew and then she reappeared.

She glanced affectionately at the boy.

Why was I afraid? Earlier she had informed me he was one of the kindest and one of the most thoughtful boys in all the world.

She carried an appliance in from the kitchen that I did not recognize, and she put it on the credenza.

Such an omen. I have asked myself what darker purpose is being served when a magician pulls his rabbit out of the hat.

I felt a tap on my back, in the middle of my back, as I hurried away, past the woman and her son, with apologies.

I had the long, uneven road to drive.

Evangeline showed up in her sporty car, where I live, on the morning of the following day.

There was something wonderful in this—it's the whole point of the story.

And we had become good friends, occasionally, for normally about an hour and a half at a time.

She said, "I am not blaming you."

My father came down the stairs, my mother, too.

Evangeline was addressing me lovingly.

Mother said, "She was married to Jerry! She's talking nonsense."

Dad said, "I didn't think you wanted us to see her."

My kitchen, where I went off to, has an island range and the beauty of this island is difficult to convey, but pesty problems can seem irrelevant when I am in the vicinity of my Viking.

I was thinking Evangeline had had her say, that she could depart now with a light heart.

When I returned to the foyer, my father was holding the newel-post, my mother—in her short, striped robe with her bare legs—was going back up the stairs.

Evangeline—and I was very moved by this—was still waiting for me and I wondered if I would rise to my own occasion.

Then my mother shouted, "They're going to clean the air conditioners first!" The Best Air van had arrived.

Eventually, Evangeline gave up with some hostility and she drove herself home.

In the meantime, I got a few payments recorded, made out bank deposits, and checked cash accounts. I think I'll be an ideal ally for somebody someday. This belief is borne in magic.

Am I not like the vanishing bead? Presto!

Place me inside of any paper cup. In due course I am in my own pocket, when I cap—carry through, or when I conclude.

WITH RED CHAIR

In the words of people who frequently repeat themselves—he is told fair words of devotion, sitting in a room decked out in antique red velvet.

Then he is miles away, say—getting a kick out of a pleasant night in a boat on sea water.

He is eating Vienna rolls with a member of the opposite sex near a roadside chapel, having a flirtation.

His recovery of an old debt reverses a disappointment. He will buy a new V-necked cardigan!

There must be something in fortune-telling. He will get tickets to the theater and only mildly suffer the experience.

This good luck was not the last, but the lucky are not always wise and he can well stand some more of it.

TRY

"Is this what you don't want?" Miss Natchez asked.

"Yes," the woman said.

"Pam!" a man said. "I have this here, if you'd like to look at it."

Pursuing him into the next room, the woman saw some other shoppers tipped into their places.

The man attended to Pam, and Miss Natchez helped out with Pam also.

They recommended something they talked her into.

. . .

Pam washed her face and her upper body at her bathroom sink when she returned home.

Better to have a full tub bath.

She unlocked the chain around her neck, disengaged herself from it, and its links spilled and then stacked themselves inside of a dish.

She gave out one of her short-hand, pitched yells when she fell short of the tub, much like a tossed child, flying through space, because of the fact that somebody didn't prefer her.

REMOVAL MEN

You have people nowadays—the men in general, who were helping the woman—and that which they should not disturb, she had put into a crate.

She put a yellow-flowered plant into the crate.

The men's names were embroidered on their shirt pockets, but truly, there was no need to address one or another of them. A question could just be asked of one—without use of a name.

The pockets of their garments were needleworks with thread in bright white. But for Marwood, somebody had devised an orange and mustard-yellow embroidery.

The woman was standing a step aside and didn't have much to contribute, but she looked at a man—at what he was making ready to take—and she held her hands with her palms turned away from her body with her fingers spread, as if she had dirtied herself.

At the curb, the woman's car was an Opel, and the hood was up, and the door to the car was out, and what was its color? It was a butterscotch and a man, up to his elbows, was under the hood. Now and again he'd go back into the car and try the starter engine. Ted—that was that one.

It could be lovely, the woman was thinking. It was already lonely and there were mountains and mosses and grasses and violent deaths nowadays, and injuries and punishments, and the woman finds the merest suggestion of cheerful companionship and carousal—a bit too dramatic.

A MERE FLASK POURED OUT

The heavily colored area—it became a shade dingier—after I knocked over her decanter and there was the sourish smell of the wine.

I saw Mother reaching toward the spill, but the time that was left to her was so scant as to be immaterial.

The little incident of the accidental spill had the fast pace of a race, hitherto neglected or unknown.

"Go home!" Mother said. And I didn't look so good to her she said. "How dare you tell me what to do—when you threw me away! You threw your brother away, too!"

Within a month, Mother was dead.

I inherited her glass carafe with its hand-cut, diamond-and-fan design, which we now use on special occasions.

We do well and we've accomplished many excellent things.

"Don't do it that way!" I had cried. My daughter had tried to uncork a bottle of wine, but since I thought it was my turn, I took it from her.

Here are other methods I use to apply heavy pressure: I ask her where she is going, what does she want, how does she know and why. She should increase her affectionate nature, be successful and happy. Mentally, she must show me she has that certain ability to try.

BANG BANG ON THE STAIR

I said, "Would you like a rope? You know that haul you have is not secured properly."

"No," he said, "but I see you have string!"

"If this comes into motion—" I said, "you should use a rope."

"Any poison ivy on that?" he asked me, and I told him my rope had been in the barn peacefully for years.

He took a length of it to the bedside table. He had no concept for what wood could endure.

"Table must have broken when I lashed it onto the truck," he said.

And, when he was moving the sewing machine, he let the cast iron wheels—bang, bang on the stair.

I had settled down to pack up the flamingo cookie jar, the cutlery, and the cookware, but stopped briefly, for how many times do you catch sudden sight of something heartfelt?

I saw our milk cows in their slow parade in the pasture and then the calf broke through with a leap from behind—its head was up, its forelegs spread.

"Don't leave!" Mother screamed at me, and she had not arrived to help me.

She tripped and fell over a floor lamp's coiled electrical cord.

There's just a basic rule of conduct that applies here—also known as a maxim—so I held out my hand.

She gripped and re-gripped my palm hard and all of my fingers before hoisting herself by pulling on me.

She kept tugging on my hand on her deathbed also for a long stretch, until she died. For don't little strokes fell great oaks?

A girl from the neighborhood rang the bell today to ask if I had a balloon. I didn't have any and I hadn't seen one in years.

"That's all you need?" I asked her. "How about some string?"

I noticed that the girl's eyes were bright and intelligent and that she was delighted, possibly with me.

I went to search where I keep a liquid-glue pen, specialty tape, and twine. I kept on talking while I pawed around for some reason in the drawer.

A LITTLE BOTTLE OF TEARS

It should have been nicer—our friendships, our travel, our romances secretly lived—if we weren't so old. But still it was an interesting situation to be in.

We all but ignored the wife's tears—which could have filled a small bottle.

And the wife was petite and well groomed and I knew why she was crying. She thought her trials were all about adultery at that time.

As the evening proceeded, the wife cheered up for some of it and her conversation was drawing us in with topics she knew we would feel comfortable talking about, because potentially our relationship could be adversarial and her husband was tending to pontificate, showing off his legal wings with paragraphs upon paragraphs.

You find yourself in a situation where you have agreed, agreed, agreed, agreed and you realize this is not such a good agreement.

How did all this end? Oh, fine, fine, fine, fine, fine—although our process of digestion—they'd served us *kartoffelpuffer* and *sauerbraten*—was not yet complete—when the husband said finally about his wife, "Bettie's tired."

To my mind—she's hysterical, sincere, easily distracted, and not adaptable. I remember when I wanted to know even more about her.

They lived only on the ground floor—the rest was rented out. A trestle table, where you could put your gloves, stood in the long hall that had stone floor tiles set on the diagonal.

Bettie's thumbs were as I remembered—heavy and clubbed—and she wore the eye-catching turquoise ring, circa 1890, with three pearls, that I knew she was proud of because I had given it to her.

"Bettie's tired," the husband repeated.

"I am tired," Bettie said.

And there was no polite way for him to tell us, "Fuck off now."

There'd be no more condescending talk, no fresh subjects, never likely an opportunity to privately reminisce with Bettie about the times when we were side by side, experiencing that alternating rhythm forward and back.

"Can we give you a lift home?"

"No, that's not necessary, we drove," we said.

I went into their bathroom to urinate before we left. I am a man, if that wasn't clear before this, and not a drunken one, not cruel—and I was holding myself then, gently—somewhat lovingly, to relieve myself.

I washed my hands and face and looked into the mirror. My face has changed so much recently. The lines of age were drawn everywhere like the marks made by a claw, and they looked to me freshly made. Then there are those growing fleshy abutments around my jaw and under my chin.

It was rainy outside and we were significantly dampened by the time we reached our car. And, in addition, a smelly ailanthus tree tossed a pitcherful of storm water—as if from a sacred fount—all over my head. There were continuing showers—it was dripping, gushy.

Still it was all so charming and heartening—that is—the summer storm, and the trees and our sky, alongside those several memories of Bettie and me.

My wife said to me en route, "Well, I suppose I'm on the wrong track, too."

Of course, it took a long time for her to go downhill, all the way down it.

Meanwhile, we became very friendly with the DePauls—Clifford and Daisy.

They lived in an apartment crammed with blue-and-white china, for one thing. I thought Daisy usually looked pensive and sad and my wife thought that her scowl meant that she detested us.

A large oil painting of a female nude—hands together as if prayerful—had been suspended over their mantel. Their apartment was in disarray.

But, there's always a moment before it all becomes okay.

WHEN I WAS OLD AND UGLY

The creature had come absurdly close to our window. It had lifted its chin—face—specifically toward mine while we were at breakfast in the country.

I'd say the animal looked and looked at me and looked, ardently.

I was reminded how to fall in love by meeting its eyes and by how long the rendezvous lasted—until doomsday, say.

I am unhappily married. Today I was dressed up in red-fox orange—orangutan orange—apricot orange, candlelight orange. I had on a wool plaid coat and had been racketing around my city precinct doing errands.

Returning home, while in the elevator of our building, facing the closed door, I combed nearly every hair—all that thinning hair along the sides of my skull.

That massive man that I didn't know at all, who had a stiffness of manner at the back of the elevator, he acknowledged me. And the doorman Bill had not averted his eyes.

No, not the sort of thing that I usually report. No, that I had withdrawn the tortoiseshell comb from my purse to do the smoothing with and then re-stowed it on the way to 3A, our apartment.

The comb I keep in the quilted sack, where I also conceal a tiny toothpaste, the easy-to-carry traveler's toothbrush, and my eyeglass-lens polishing cloth.

The carpet was unmarked by dirt, but one important thing in our foyer was missing—the color with the green leaves in a vase. The old floor gets better with age, but boy it needed to be cleaned up—then it will shine.

I also have affectionate and friendly wishes for the brass, crystal, silver dishes, vases and pitchers.

My conversation with my husband was as follows: "Are you all right? What do you want? You're looking at me."

In the park I had wanted to talk today to a bird who wasn't interested in talking to me.

Lust and temptation are sometimes personified. I heard the bird cry—*Chew! Chew!* I took pains to say *Chew! Chew!*—loudly, too.

PALM AGAINST PALM

It is a pity there is also the nature of the surface of the skin—combined with the error of her eyes and the divots at the centers of her breasts.

Her tiny skirt is much like a figure skater's skirt that may—as she lets her legs fling forward to walk—flap.

Clap. Clap.

The girl—to get here—goes in the direction of the vanishing point, on up the steep grade.

These living quarters with the man, that she has entered, are bordered in the front by bluet and merrybells and by the myrtle and foam flowers at the back.

Her exit requires her to go through a door that shuts, ta-ta!—with those two little beats of sound.

Come along!—for wonderful it may seem that those hills are presenting themselves not just as technical details or as small regions near the tollway.

Did she see those birds that were falling like leaves?—the leaves that were flying like birds?

The girl will extend herself to travel and to sway beyond the sweepgate into somebody else's household and she will hurry to meet up with somebody.

So when she arrives at the northern suburb, she finds a high house with a heavy gate. There is a seat near the door.

Whose house is this?

There is a tent bed, a hearth, and a sectional bookcase.

"At least I don't keep people waiting. Am I doing everything?" the girl asks.

"Hey!"

"Now look at you."

Then she was pulling her blouse together and she went to get a glass of water, a pot of coffee.

The brightly scaled moon was rising, but this girl never became a well-liked businesswoman with a growing family in the community.

Neither is she endowed with any remarkable qualities. We

never spoke of her specialized skills or of her inclination to be otherwise. My fault. Go fuck herself. Apology accepted.

HUMAN COMB

A pastel portrait of the deceased Mrs. Meldrum senior, as a young girl, was placed over a console table with flared legs, and I stared at Mrs. Meldrum's face and got to know her, for no purpose, for no benefit, none. But like a bird, I might have been eating out of her hand!

Her son, Melvyn, had forgotten he'd invited us. And thank you, Melvyn, for that. He suggested gin, rum, Scotch, rye, sherry, schnapps, Pepsi, cold tea, or beer.

And here I was in the company of a private detective and other pet owners. Some of them became scornful when the conversation centered on the next election or on Melvyn Meldrum's unsympathetic mother and what was really so bad about her.

And even though I have no teeth—they'd all been pulled, because I was set to get implants and my dentures were just too painful to wear—I consumed a Diet Pepsi and some soft pizza topping.

This is not to say I am old. Far from it! Sometimes I just go to any lengths—and I had gotten started clearing out my God-given, skimpy, and in some cases, my diseased teeth.

So Melvyn had come to the door dead drunk and had told us we might as well come in for a drink. And where was his wife Yvonne, just then? She was upstairs getting ready for a different social event.

Yvonne Meldrum, when she appeared, brought in a tray of Limburger cheese, saltines, and Cheddar Goldfish.

And, I don't forget what has happened to my pal Jack—he was there—a man I'd once had a fine time with—with my legs hanging up over his shoulders.

I wrote a note to the Meldrums after our return that it was so lovely to see you, so much fun. It was a joy.

Did Melvyn's wife Yvonne leave him? Had she planned on finding somebody else to take her by the breasts? Because that night, while we ate, when June Hockett said, "Get Yvonne," we discovered that Yvonne had left the premises!

I believe that this incident occurred before Vic's and my son was born—soon after my divorce from Jack.

Had I been unhappy with Jack? Well, certainly Jack had been very woebegone.

One of the little girls at the party played a child's version of a sad song on the spinet piano, while the other younger girl came up behind her to spoil it.

Vic said, as we went out for a taxi, "That was fun." He stood just beyond the curb, stretching his arm out and by and by we arrived at our hotel.

Back in New Paltz, the next day, I needed to, but I could not go to the post office, but I could groom our dog Demon because it was Labor Day.

When I comb out Demon's hair I may use a human comb and I always get under his belly. Sometimes I use an undercoat rake. I don't ever use medicated shampoo for the genital area. And, I don't need to imagine the pain of any teeth rotting out of Demon's head!—so I let the vet tend to that.

But I have never had any discussion with Vic about whether he, Vic, is actually a jealous spouse—or about what happened to Yvonne.

I am unemotional about the abrupt ending of friendships and there'd be no purpose, no benefit, none, to exploring these subjects further—such as: have I come clean enough?

I am—yes—utterly at ease in the company of others, secretive, sexually active, quite adaptable.

And many have said of me, I hear—She's very charming.

The following stories have appeared in *Harper's*: "A Little Bottle of Tears," "Living Deluxe," "Girl with a Pencil," "A Gray Pottery Head," "With Red Chair," "Head of the Big Man."

These stories first appeared, sometimes in a slightly different form or with a different title, in the *American Reader*: "Try," "How Blown Up"; in *Granta*: "Specialist"; in *La Granada*: "Gulls," "Of the True and Final Good"; in *The Lifted Brow*: "The Mermaid Pose," "Glimpses of Mrs. Williams," The Skol"; in *London Review of Books*: "Lamb Chops, Cod," "Perform Small Tasks," "Removal Men"; in *PANK*: "Lavatory"; in *Queen Mob's Tea House*: "There Is Always a Hesitation Before Turning in a Finished Job"; in *Salt Hill*: "Flying Things"; in *Tammy*: "Palm Against Palm"; in *Tin House*: "At a Period of Exceptional Dullness," "A Mere Flask Poured Out," "Sigh"; in *Unsaid*: "Head of a Naked Girl"; in *VICE*: "Cinch," "Greed," "Personal Details," "The Thickening Wish," "When I Was Old and Ugly"; in *The White Review*: "Love, Beauty, and Vanity Itself."

"A Mere Flask Poured Out" was reprinted in *The Best Small Fictions 2015*.

ABOUT THE AUTHOR

Diane Williams is the author of eight books, including a collection of her selected stories. She is also the founder and editor of the literary annual *NOON*, which is acclaimed both in America and abroad.